BOOK 1
Short
A

DISNEY · PIXAR
RATATOUILLE
(rat·a·too·ee)

Rat in a Hat

ISBN: 978-1-338-12826-0

10 9 8 7 6 5 4 3 2 1   16 17 18 19 20

Printed in Malaysia 106

First Printing, September 2016

Scholastic Inc.

Look **at that rat!**

That rat has a spatula.

That rat can use a **pan**.

That rat is a natural!

Look **at that man**!

That man can not cook.

That man's food
is very **bad**.

Look! **That man can catch that rat.**

The **man** **has** a **plan**.

The **rat can** give him a **hand**!

The **rat** helps the **man**.

The **man** learns from the **rat**.

The **man** hides the **rat**…

in his **hat**!

Imagine **that!**